Lady Pancake & Sir French Toast

To Chloe & Declan, who always put the bottle of syrup back in the fridge . . .
no matter how few drops are left. —J.F.

For my parents who encouraged me to draw pictures rather than write a CV. —B.K.

ISBN 978-1-338-04484-3

Text copyright © 2015 by Josh Funk. Illustrations copyright © 2015 by Brendan Kearney.
All rights reserved. Published by Scholastic Inc., 557 Broadway, New York, NY 10012,
by arrangement with Sterling Publishing Co., Inc. SCHOLASTIC and associated logos are
trademarks and/or registered trademarks of Scholastic Inc.

The publisher does not have any control over and does not assume any responsibility for
author or third-party websites or their content.

12 11 10 9 8 7 6 5 4 3 2 1   16 17 18 19 20 21

Printed in the U.S.A.   40

First Scholastic printing, April 2016

The artwork for this book was created using pencils and digital media.
Designed by Andrea Miller

Lady Pancake & Sir French Toast

by JOSH FUNK   illustrated by BRENDAN KEARNEY

SCHOLASTIC INC.

Deep in the fridge and behind the green peas,
way past the tofu and left of the cheese,

up in the corner, and back by a roast,
sat Lady Pancake beside Sir French Toast.

The leftover friends were as close as could be,
until they heard news from their neighbor, Miss Brie.
"The syrup is almost completely all gone!
A single drop's left! Just a drop!" she went on.

"The last drop is mine!"
Lady Pancake conversed.

But French Toast replied,
"Not if I get there first!"

Like that, he was off, and the race had begun,
with Pancake behind, breaking into a run.

Through Broccoli Forest, past Orange Juice Fountain,
they climbed to the top of Potato Mash Mountain.

Pushing and shoving, they fought for the lead,
Toast behind Pancake, who rolled at high speed.

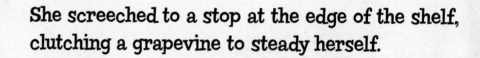

She screeched to a stop at the edge of the shelf, clutching a grapevine to steady herself.

Toast didn't notice and couldn't quite stop,
plummeting down into jam with a . . .

PLOP!

He scraped himself off
and yelled up, "You're a meanie!"
as Pancake rappelled
down a rope of linguini.

She bragged, "I'm the best of all breakfast food treats!"
then hurdled a lime and skipped over two beets.

"*I am!*" thought Toast, but his chances looked bleak.
So Toast took a shortcut down Sauerkraut Peak.
Skiing past spinach and artichoke dip,
Toast vaulted high in the air with a . . .

FLIP!

Nearing the edge he tried one final jump
but stumbled and fell way below with a . . .

THUMP!

Pancake made use of her seafaring skills
and sailed across oceans of soup, causing spills.

But Chili Lagoon slathered Pancake in muck.
And then at a fork in the road she got stuck.

"Don't go that way!"
yelled a chickpea to warn her.

But Pancake sped on
and got trapped in a corner!

Caught behind dressings, one Russian, one Ranch,
she squeezed out and started a bean . . .

AVALANCHE!

Toast reemerged
in the vegetable crisper,
sneaking up swiftly,
not making a whisper.

Beans were now falling
from such a great height—
Some kidney, some lima,
some pinto, some white!

Searching for safety from raining legumes,
Toast turned to hide but was blasted by fumes
of Brussels sprouts left from an old party platter.

So quickly he climbed up a celery ladder.

Beside him a lettuce leaf parachute landed.
Pancake flipped out. "It is mine!" she demanded.

Battered and soggy, exhausted and crumbling,
too tired to push, they were limping and stumbling.

There stood the bottle of syrup at last . . .

But wait . . . it was empty! They stood quite aghast.

Licking his lips with a sneer that was awful,
out of the shadows crept Baron von Waffle.

"I got here first while you boasted and bickered.
My, was that syrup delicious," he snickered.

With one evil laugh, Waffle slipped out of sight.
The syrup was gone. No more reason to fight.

Trudging back home beneath layers of grime,
Toast said, "Perhaps we should *not* fight next time."

"Agreed," replied Pancake. "As friends we should share.
Hey, look! We can split up that butter right there. . . ."